T0362927

Sandcastles

A story by Louis White

Published by
White Tiger Media Productions Pty Ltd
Tel: +61 2 9220 1722
M: +61 (0)423 410 388
E: louis.white@whitetigermedia.com.au
W: www.whitetigermedia.com.au

First printed in Sydney, Australia in July 2013.

Second print run by Peachy Print Australia, September 2022.

Peachy Print Australia Pty Ltd
6/1 Hordern Place
Camperdown NSW 2050 Australia
www.peachyprint.com.au

Louis White asserts the moral rights to be identified as the author of this work.
Website: www.louiswhite.com

Damon Taylor asserts the illustrations and cover design copyrights of this work.
www.damonillus.com

This book is a work of fiction. All the characters in this book are fictitious and any resemblance
to actual persons, living or dead, is purely coincidental.

National Library of Australia Cataloguing-in-Publication entry
Author: Louis White, ca. 1968-

Book design and illustration: Damon Taylor

Title: Sandcastles

ISBN 978-0-646-90314-9 (paperback)

Dewey Number: A823.4

This book is dedicated to Princess Buttercup.

May she one day find the courage to let go of the past

and look to the future with hope.

Day 1: Sunday
(Childhood)

Mary-Anne was tired. She was always tired. Despite the fact that the sun was shining, there was blue sky outside and it was just a stone's throw to the ocean, she felt no enthusiasm for the day.

She had been lazing in bed all day like a sloth and avoiding contact with any human being except through her phone.

Mary-Anne loved her phone and couldn't go five minutes without checking to see if someone had emailed or texted her. Even if she didn't respond, she liked to know that people needed her. It made her feel important, and without it, she could not see how she could possibly function. Her phone was her lifeline.

It was now getting into the late afternoon, and Mary-Anne could hear the streets were still buzzing with the sound of summer approaching. She decided she should leave the comfort of her bed and at least look outside. After all, what harm could it do? And her phone would be in her hand all the time.

The big house she lived in was empty. All the guests and family members had left for the day to go outside and have some fun. But Mary-Anne was far too busy and important to waste a whole day having fun. I mean, what if she got a very important call or email and wasn't able to respond? No, she couldn't go an hour without the need to be on her phone.

As Mary-Anne looked out the window, she saw a rainbow lorikeet. She was amazed at its beauty and, letting her phone slip onto the table, she momentarily forgot about her very important world. Unlike most rainbow lorikeets, this bird had no partner and didn't make a noise, and it seemed to be staring straight at her.

Carefully and slowly, Mary-Anne opened the patio doors to

get closer to this wonderful creature. The closer she got, the more the bird seemed to stare straight at her, and Mary-Anne was fascinated by its colours – bright green, red, blue and yellow.

She was within a metre of the bird when it turned and flew up and slightly to the left, swirling around and looking down at Mary-Anne, as if to invite her to follow.

Mary-Anne followed the rainbow lorikeet down the side path of the house and out to the street. She walked slowly behind the bird; it was never more than five metres from her and never made a sound. She soon lost track of where she was, away from the crowds and walking along an unfamiliar path. Where was she going?

She had lost all concept of time. Was it five minutes or an hour she had been walking? Nonetheless, her interest in the rainbow lorikeet had not diminished. Its colours were mesmerising, and she couldn't take her eyes away from it. It was like she was in a trance.

Suddenly, the rainbow lorikeet took off, squawking loudly. Mary-Anne's head spun round and round as she tried to follow its circles in the sky, but soon the bird had disappeared. Mary-Anne caught her breath and looked around to see where she was.

Much to her amazement, she was standing on a secluded beach she had never seen before. It was as beautiful as one could imagine. The sand was white and pristine, the ocean bluer than blue and the skies looked friendlier than ever. What a magical place she had discovered, and she had it all to herself.

She couldn't stop smiling.

She had started to walk slowly along the beach, soaking in its loveliness, when she saw something in the distance. She was unsure at first, but upon closer inspection, she realised someone was making a sandcastle.

Mary-Anne increased her pace and saw a little blond, blue-eyed boy with a spade and bucket digging away at the sand.

"What are you doing?" she asked.

"Building a sandcastle," said the boy as he diligently went about his work.

"What kind of sandcastle are you building?"

"A big one with plenty of rooms."

The boy had not deviated from his task and continued to fill and empty the bucket and shape the sandcastle with his hands. He had not once looked up at Mary-Anne, who stood watching, admiring the pleasure the boy was taking from his craft, until the boy stopped.

"I've finished my first room," he said proudly. "Come and have a look."

Mary-Anne smiled and bent over as the boy retreated into the background.

She pretended to look inside the window and admire his craftsmanship, but the boy said, "You need to look inside the window properly."

Mary-Anne smiled again, this time more out of politeness, but also out of respect for what the boy had built, she got down on one knee and peered inside the window.

From there, Mary-Anne was transported into her childhood.

The room was full of images and memories, from when she was a baby through to her early teenage years.

But Mary-Anne didn't see a child; she saw an adult pretending to be a child. She saw music lessons, language lessons, school lessons, religious lessons, sport lessons, and in fact, everything was a lesson. All around her adults were telling her what to do and giving constant instruction on what she should be doing all the time.

Suddenly, the rainbow lorikeet appeared beside her. "Now, Mary-Anne, do you see what we have here?"

Mary-Anne couldn't understand what was happening but thought it best just to nod.

"Your childhood was a complex childhood. Your loving parents wanted you to explore your talents through hard work and discipline, as did your teachers, because they thought they knew what was best for you. They wanted structure and a future for you that they considered to be in your best interests.

"But doesn't the child already know more than the adult? Doesn't the child already know what is right and wrong?

"What tastes good and what doesn't? What they like doing and what they don't? What makes them happy and what makes them sad? Doesn't a child simply fall asleep when tired rather than fight through it as adults do?"

"The child's conscience is clear and innocent and is only corrupted by adults. Children are naturally curious and want to explore all in front of them to see what something feels and tastes like. They want to discover the endless possibilities of a new-found object.

"Adults around the world need to let children learn through their natural curiosity of objects, animals, foods and the like, as their brains develop and encompass all that is around while assisting them with guidance and understanding.

"Most childhoods around the world involve structured learning – some natural, some forced – from a young age. But

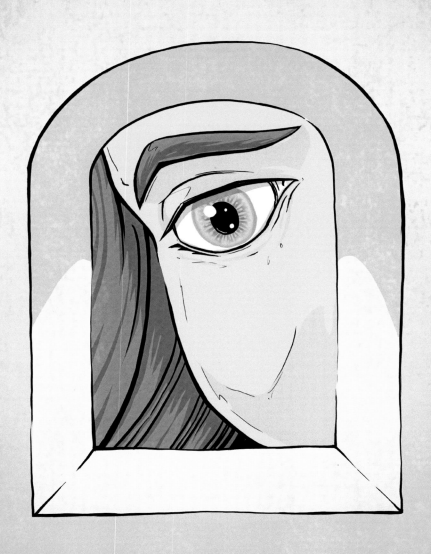

we must let a child be a child and children be children. There must be spontaneity, and there must be time for a child to simply explore on its own with no adult present.

"Yes, there is love and nurturing for children, but often it is misplaced, and this has left many children misplaced in the world today. It is not too late for adults to change their teaching methods."

Mary-Anne looked up at the rainbow lorikeet, who soon started speaking directly to her.

"All is not lost," the bird said. "Those disciplines you learned as a child can serve you well today in other areas, and that spontaneity you so badly crave is within you at any second.

"The silliness, the random laughter, the craziness, the freedom that every child seeks is very much within you and is part of you, and as you know, has been recently activated.

"Never forget the foundations upon which one has been built and never forget that they can be used to benefit you in later life in different forms, even though it may not be obvious at the time."

With those final words, the rainbow lorikeet flew away, and Mary-Anne was suddenly standing alone on the beach far away from the sandcastle. She looked around and couldn't see the boy and wondered what had happened. Was it a dream?

Mary-Anne suddenly grew weary and felt the need to lie down. As she turned to her right, she saw a beautiful big oak tree surrounded by fresh green grass. She couldn't believe her luck as it was only a short distance away.

She walked in a leisurely way to the oak tree, trying to comprehend what had just happened. She lay beneath the tree and found it very comfortable. Soon, she was fast asleep.

Day 2: Monday
(Escapism)

Mary-Anne awoke feeling restless and unsure whether yesterday had actually happened or if it was a dream. She looked in the mirror and told herself she was far too serious a person to believe that a rainbow lorikeet had shown her a secluded beach and a boy had built a sandcastle with a secret room that took her back to her past. No, that hadn't happened, and it was time to come to her senses.

What was she thinking? It was now time to get on with her adult life and very important job. Of course, that started as soon as she woke up, checking her emails from all around the world and listening to her voicemail messages. No time to respond to friends' texts or emails; they weren't a priority.

Mary-Anne drove to work in her very expensive car, calling work colleagues, checking her emails and organising her very busy life. Oh my, she thought, how do I get this all done? No one could ever be as busy as me.

She weaved in and out of traffic before duly parking her car and ordering her first coffee for the day. No, Mary-Anne couldn't function without her morning coffee. She set to work straight away.

All day, she was running from one meeting to the next, writing this report, organising that conference, planning a business trip. No one's time was as precious as hers. All day, she ignored personal emails, texts and phone calls from friends and family.

Mary-Anne was driving to another very important meeting at the end of the day when a client called to tell her it had been cancelled. As she was near her current place of residence, she decided to call in at home and work the rest of the day locked away in her bedroom. There would be no time for dinner because she was far too important for that.

Mary-Anne took one set of bags inside and was coming back out for her laptop, when she saw a noisy miner sitting on her car bonnet. Mary-Anne's natural reaction was to shoo the bird away, but once again, she found herself fascinated by a creature so small yet so powerful.

Like the rainbow lorikeet, the noisy miner stared straight at her, not making a sound. Its yellow beak and grey and white feathers defined a creature of purpose. Its protruding chest portrayed an image of strength as it leaned forward.

As Mary-Anne approached, the bird took off, looking back at her, encouraging her to follow. She forgot where she was and watched the bird fly high in the sky.

Like a child with a new toy, she followed the bird, losing all track of time and not sure where she was going but unable to take her eyes off the noisy miner.

No bird came near the noisy miner, and it looked to be all-powerful in the sky despite its diminutive size.

Soon she was back upon the same secluded beach as yesterday with its white, pristine sand and clear blue ocean with barely a whimper of a wave. How did I end up here again?

She looked left and then right and started walking in the latter direction. Then once again, she stumbled upon the blond, blue-eyed boy building his sandcastle.

"Hello," Mary-Anne said again, smiling.

"Hello back," said the boy. Just like yesterday, he did not stop working. His sandcastle had grown.

"Why are you wearing work clothes?" the boy asked. "Hardly appropriate for the beach."

Mary-Anne looked down and realised that her pants, blouse and high heels were not appropriate for the beach at all. She had almost forgotten that she had been unloading the car to continue to work in her bedroom.

"Yes, that is a good question," she responded. "I didn't intend to come to the beach at all. You see, I was taking out some files from my car when…" But Mary-Anne stopped talking when she realised that the boy wasn't listening.

She decided it was best to ask him some questions.

"I see you have been busily toiling away," Mary-Anne stated.

The boy did not respond.

"How big will your sandcastle be?"

The boy did not look up.

Mary-Anne stood silently watching, thinking it was probably time to walk away. She had just started to turn her body around when the boy exclaimed with joy, "Aha! I've finished the second room. You really need to look inside this new window. I think you will find it very interesting."

Mary-Anne looked at the boy, who met her gaze. His eyes were a translucent blue. She felt as though he was looking at her soul. She felt a shiver run through her body.

She couldn't hold his gaze and averted her eyes to the second room of the sandcastle and looked inside the window.

Immediately, the fun of her childhood appeared before her eyes with horses, goats, spiders, dogs, cats, snakes and almost every living creature upon the earth going past one by one.

"Do you remember this?" the noisy miner asked, sitting on her shoulder. Mary-Anne nodded in agreement.

"Do you remember catching creatures great and small, setting them free again and then chasing them for fun? Do you remember as a very young child jumping on the back of a horse and riding as fast as the wind? Do you remember hours playing with dogs and cats and never being bored?

"Do you remember the peace and happiness the animals gave you? We could all learn so much from the simple life of animals.

"These animals were there to teach you a lesson about life, a life you have forgotten about since you moved to the city and forgot about your roots.

"Look at the innocence and playfulness of animals. Feel their warmth, their hunger and their desire. Look at how they enjoy the simple things of life – eating, drinking, sleeping, playing and lovemaking.

"We are just as simple as they are, yet we tend to forget and ignore that what we learned as children is still very applicable today. Why don't you like to live this way anymore, Mary-Anne? Why must you be so serious all the time and forget to have fun and explore the earth the way you used to?"

Mary-Anne had gone from smiling broadly to suddenly being pensive. It was a good question, she thought.

"It is not too late to regain the enthusiasm of your youth," the noisy miner said. "You are still very young at heart and young in age, even though you feel weary. Seek out those who bring you laughter and joy and hold them near to your heart; otherwise, you will grow old very fast. Seek out those who will take you back to your roots because they want the best for you, not because it is now convenient."

And with those words, the noisy miner departed.

Mary-Anne looked up to see once again she was some distance from the sandcastle and the boy was nowhere to be seen. She turned around to see the beautiful old oak tree in all its glory with its loving branches and leaves showing the last days of spring.

The grass looked equally inviting, and she lay down between the glorious roots of the old oak tree and could have sworn that they had moved closer together and were smoother than yesterday.

That was the last thought in her head before sleep had its way.

Day 3 Tuesday
(The lost years)

Mary-Anne awoke feeling contented but strange. Once again, she was unsure of what had happened. She wanted to talk to her sister, but her sister was nowhere to be found. This big old house had many rooms, and even though Mary-Anne searched every one of them, she couldn't find her sister anywhere.

But that was enough of that, and it was time for her to start getting serious again about her very important job. There were all sorts of personal emails, texts and phone calls she had ignored asking her to this function and that, but Mary-Anne was too busy to answer them.

She always arrived at functions unannounced and at the last minute. As long as there was plenty of alcohol, she would be there and be the life of the party. She knew she was charming and pretty and that men always chased after her no matter how much her appearance changed. She loved the attention even though she feigned disinterest. Men always wanted her even when she didn't want them, or so she said.

Mary-Anne started her car and took off for the drive to the office, making phone calls and checking emails and texts along the way. She was always multi-tasking because she was a very important person with very important work to do. But at the back of her mind, Mary-Anne couldn't help thinking that something in her life was starting to change.

In her first meeting, she listened, but not as assiduously as previously. She wrote her first report, but not with the same intensity as others. She planned her next fortnight of work, but not with the same rigour as in the past.

While she still thought her work very important, something else was beginning to become important too, but she could

not figure out what. It would come to her, she thought, as the
nagging feeling stayed with her all day.

Mary-Anne left work and, surprisingly, found the traffic easy
to navigate. She was home in no time, and the sun was shining.
It was actually a glorious day, and she decided to take advantage
of the remaining hours of sunshine by going for a run.

She changed quickly because there was no time to waste.
Mary-Anne was always in a hurry, and she couldn't be away
from her phone for too long in case some important message
needed to be responded to.

She put on her sports cap, sports bra, T-shirt, shorts, socks
and trainers and started running. No birds to distract me
today, she thought. She started slowly and built up her speed
before, after a couple of kilometres, deciding to stretch.

Mary-Anne was busily stretching her calves, when she
looked down and saw a yellow robin. She was only one metre
away from a bird that was notoriously hard to get close to.

The yellow robin looked up at Mary-Anne and held her gaze.

With a worm in its beak quickly swallowed, the yellow robin jumped onto her shoulder and looked straight ahead.

Mary-Anne knew it was time to start running.

The yellow robin flew off a short distance ahead of her and slightly above her line of sight, and Mary-Anne was transfixed on the bird.

Mary-Anne had found her second wind, and it didn't matter what obstacle was put in front of her – hill, gate, path, dirt – she managed to navigate it.

All the while, the yellow robin, with its yellow chest and grey back and head, was flying up and down and all around Mary-Anne. Never once was the bird intimidated by her presence and seemed to almost smile the closer it got to her.

But then, all of a sudden, the bird flew off and into the distance. Mary-Anne whirled around, trying to locate it, but all to no avail. She looked down to see the clear white sands and beautiful blue ocean and knew exactly where she was.

She hurriedly walked down the beach to see the blue-eyed, blond boy building his sandcastle, which had grown substantially since yesterday.

"Wow, this is beginning to look impressive," Mary-Anne exclaimed. "How big will it finally be?"

The boy did not look at Mary-Anne. He simply continued building.

"I am not quite finished yet," the boy said to her. "But you are all sweaty, and you have the ocean waiting right there for you. Why don't you swim?"

Mary-Anne was about to argue, which was something that she was very good at and did all day at work and with friends, lovers (old and new) and family, but decided that this time, she would simply hold her tongue and take his advice.

She stripped down to her underwear and jumped into the ocean. The water was perfect, the waves negligible and the vision underneath so clear it felt as if she was wearing a diving mask.

A school of fish swam nearby, and as she rose to the surface, two dolphins were playing.

When she returned from her swim, she saw the boy standing proudly over his growing sandcastle. He had a bright bubbly smile, and it made her smile broadly too.

"What do you have to show me this time?" Mary-Anne asked. The boy simply pointed at the third room.

Mary-Anne looked at the boy and then looked at the new room and bent down to peek in the window, where a world of parties, travel and good times flowed.

She was transported from one party to another, never without a drink in her hand, along with a string of outfits and with different boyfriends.

"I imagine you have trouble remembering all of this," the yellow robin said with a frown on its beak. Mary-Anne laughed out loud.

"Some of that behaviour still carries on today," the yellow robin said, looking stern. "While it is good to express yourself and experiment, you delayed a lot of your learning potential back then with endless partying. They were the formative years of your brain development, and you wanted to regress from your problems and forget about the seriousness of life, so you took the easy option, as most human beings do today.

"Abuse of the body does nobody any favours, and ultimately, all you are doing is burying problems that will manifest in a different form. You also stayed too long in relationships that were not right for you. That is a lesson you have had trouble heeding.

"You need to understand that love comes in many forms, and it is soul-destroying to be in any relationship for the wrong reasons.

"Human beings waste so much of their lives not wanting to acknowledge who they really are, when the truth is that they are all beautiful people with goodness within. They want to experiment with their minds and bodies and bury things that society teaches them not to talk about, but they are the very things that they should talk about.

"They don't let themselves heal naturally; they waste their formative, crucial learning years partying, doing almost anything they can to stunt their development. Why?"

Mary-Anne was reflective, looking down at the sand. The yellow robin continued.

"With luck, you have now seen what the past can do to you, and what you need to do to address the imbalance in your life in the present and the future," the bird said.

"Work is one thing, play another, abuse something else altogether. Yes, you had fun in the past, and you certainly knew how to party, but it came at a cost. You are paying for that now. Remember, too much of anything leads to a lack of appreciation. You must seek balance."

Mary-Anne found herself thinking deeply after this experience and immediately headed for the old oak tree once the memories and the yellow robin had disappeared.

"Can you hear me, old oak tree?" she asked quietly, standing near the trunk. Mary-Anne looked up and down the tree, admiring its beauty, and wondered how many stories it had to tell.

She grabbed some fallen leaves and rubbed them in her hands. She smelled the red roses growing around the roots and plucked some white daisies. She felt peace and laid her head against the trunk of the tree.

Mary-Anne hoped this feeling would last for some time yet.

Day 4 : Wednesday
(Old loves)

The alarm woke Mary-Anne, but for once, she decided to turn it off. Her very important job could wait. She had slept well and wanted to continue sleeping.

It was another thirty minutes or so later when the maid came in and accidentally woke her up. The maid apologised profusely, but Mary-Anne, for once, wasn't overly concerned. She quickly showered and dressed and jumped into the car.

She decided today that she would take only urgent phone calls and not check emails and texts while driving. In between, she would listen to some soothing classical music.

She felt like listening to the piano and was calmed by the music of Frédéric Chopin and Ludwig van Beethoven.

The day seemed to pass smoothly enough and, surprisingly, Mary-Anne didn't seem too fazed whenever something didn't go her way. She could feel herself remembering the pleasant aspects of her childhood combined with the serenity of the beach.

Where is that beach? She tried searching on Google but to no avail. She decided to leave work early and search for it physically. She parked her car at home and started to walk through the streets. She replaced her high heels with flat shoes and was thoroughly enjoying the fresh air.

Mary-Anne had almost given up the search, when she tripped on a stone and fell on the grass. As she looked up, a satin bowerbird sat above her on a branch. It was alone, without its family.

It flew down and landed on her arm. This is a first, Mary-Anne thought. The satin bowerbird, with its preference for blue objects, flew off into the sky, with Mary-Anne following.

The satin bowerbird, with its striking glossy blue-back

plumage, pale bluish-white bill and violet-blue eyes, flew off a short distance ahead, never once looking back. It was almost as though it knew Mary-Anne would follow.

The journey today, however, seemed shorter than usual, or perhaps that was because Mary-Anne knew where she was heading.

Sure enough, she watched the bird fly out of sight, and before she knew it, Mary-Anne was at the beach. She wondered what today would bring and what she would learn.

She took off her shoes, slowly turned and started walking in the sand, enjoying the feeling between her toes. It was so soft. She slowed her walk and zigzagged up the beach while humming a tune. She was enjoying being silly.

For the first time all week, the blond, blue-eyed boy looked up upon her arrival. But he wasn't smiling, and this immediately caught Mary-Anne's eye.

"Today, I've finished my fourth room, and as you can see, my castle is getting bigger by the day. Soon, I will be completely finished," the boy said matter-of-factly.

"The room you will look into today has two windows, but you only need to look into one to understand the message."

With that, Mary-Anne dropped to her knees and peered in, and there she saw every ex-lover and their current lives and loves. Some were happy; some were not. Some had children; others did not.

But as she looked at each man, she was startled and alarmed that each looked her straight back in the eye.

"Frightening, isn't it?" the satin bowerbird said, landing on her hand.

"And what is the common theme with all of them, Mary-Anne?" he asked.

He could tell by the look of shock on her face that she knew the answer.

"That all of them have moved on with their lives. Some

are grateful for the time you spent together, while others you did help have forgotten that. Each one possesses a myriad of feelings about their relationship with you.

"Some harp on the negative, as this makes it easier to forget the good times and put the relationship in perspective. Others remember the good times but keep the memory closed in a box so as not to spoil the present.

"But, ultimately, most have simply moved on. They have found new love, new hope and new life.

"All of these relationships resemble good and bad memories from your past. In every adult relationship, there is at least one element of dishonesty, selfishness, temptation, greed, gluttony, envy and wrath.

"Some mistreated you, and some you mistreated, albeit in very different ways.

"All of these relationships have served a purpose, and you have learned lessons, as they have.

"But what you must learn today is to let go of the past. Forgive yourself and forgive others. That is the right thing to do, no matter how painful.

"You need to let go of the disappointment, betrayal, self-sacrifice and love that you gave in order to heal yourself and let new love into your life.

"While you hold on to old love, your heart is weak and beats at a slower pace. When you clear your heart of old love, the energy and vitality start to flow back into your life, giving you a clear mind and conscience.

"You start to breathe more easily and see life more clearly. This allows you to fully embrace new love, and in return, new love can fully embrace you. When your heart is fully open, all new possibilities flow to you."

Mary-Anne was very sad and started to cry. She had only wanted the best for each partner and was always unsure of how to leave.

"You have to extricate yourself from the past. It needs to remain in the past. All the relationships happened for a reason, but it is time to let go and heal yourself."

Mary-Anne was crying steadily now. The satin bowerbird jumped on her nose, causing her to go cross-eyed and laugh. The bird then flew to the window and said to Mary-Anne in a soft voice, "The good news is that each partner benefited from your kindness and generosity. Not that most will admit to it, as they are too busy living their current lives, but you did pass on many wonderful qualities, and some of those have been inherited.

"The lesson today is to understand that it is time to move forward with your life. Embrace what you have now and let it fully into your life.

"You have imparted a lot of love in the world and that will always be intact. Just remember, in the future, be honest about your feelings at the outset and stay true to your beliefs and people will respect you even more than they do now."

With that, the satin bowerbird disappeared, and Mary-Anne found herself standing near the old oak tree. She walked up and hugged the old tree for what seemed like an eternity.

"Tell me you love me," she pleaded, sobbing. She could have sworn she heard the tree groan as she tried to stretch her arms around its huge trunk.

She slipped down the tree and crumbled at its base.

Day 5: Thursday
(Letting go of the past)

Mary-Anne woke from a deep sleep. She was feeling sorry for herself and not at all interested in her very important job. For the first time, she started to think about how much she wanted to stay in this job. She had been with the same company for a long time now, and there weren't many challenges left.

Even though she had the respect of all those who mattered, the challenges were starting to wear thin. The constant travel, dinners, drinks and endless conventions were taking their toll. She needed time out.

She dressed slowly and drove under the speed limit throughout the whole of her journey to work, all the time participating in a conference call transmitted to four different countries.

The workday progressed slowly, and she couldn't wait for it to end. Unfortunately, she couldn't leave early due to back-to-back meetings. She had no desire to work anymore upon the day's end and couldn't get hold of her new love. She wondered what he was up to.

She decided to call her friends and family on the way home. She felt better for hearing their voices and even managed to laugh a little. She decided that it was time to find balance in her life and spend more time with them.

She stopped the car along the main beach and gazed out into the sunshine. Only two more days to summer, but already the temperature had risen.

Mary-Anne had looked down to start the car when a black-faced cuckoo-shrike appeared in her side-view mirror. She was taken aback by the darkness of its face complemented by the grey feathers of its body.

The black-faced cuckoo-shrike turned its head quickly from side to side and then looked back at Mary-Anne. She knew the drill.

Once again, she followed this delightful bird, but this time, it wasn't so much the dips and turns and sounds of the bird that captivated her as the sky above. For the first time in a long time, she realised that there was a lot more to the universe than the small world she lived in.

Mary-Anne had lost sight of living and was too focused on day-to-day survival. She had forgotten the existence of real life and had concentrated all her energy into her work.

No one else received half as much attention, and even in times when she lost herself in her new lover for a short period, it was exactly that: a short period before her mind raced back to the clock.

What was the point of earning all that money, and the stress that went with it, when you didn't live the life you wanted to?

Why was she devoting sixty to seventy hours a week of her life to work when her health, happiness and motivation for life were all suffering as a consequence? Had she become brainwashed by society's desire for always wanting more rather than being happy with what we just have?

By the time Mary-Anne turned her eyes from the clouds, she was back at the beach. This time, however, she decided to walk along the edge of the water and feel the cool ocean on her feet. It was soothing. She looked up and down and started to appreciate all that was before and behind her.

As she approached the little boy, she realised that every day he wore the same clothes – white shorts and yellow T-shirt. They never changed. He was always barefoot and very engrossed in his work. His blond hair was always ruffled and his olive skin slightly tanned.

His attention to detail was second to none, and she had started to notice little things on the castle such as a drawbridge, doors, and an outer perimeter wall that let the sea in to surround the castle, to form a barrier.

There were lookout areas at the top of each tower and a fort all around. There wasn't much that the boy hadn't thought of, and Mary-Anne was very impressed.

"Is there a dungeon and secret tunnels too?" she asked with a big smile. She wanted to know more about the boy. However, she realised he was not there to answer her questions but to guide her to somewhere or someone she was as yet unsure of.

"Now, I think you will like my fifth room," the boy said proudly. "It is somewhat unusually designed, as you can see by the shape, and some may not like it, but once you are inside, you will be amazed by its depth and size."

Mary-Anne bent down and peered inside and immediately felt surrounded by love. In fact, every which way she turned, all she could feel was love. Everyone she had touched in her life was in this room – the new, the old, the forgotten and those that had passed from this life. They were all in the room, walking, talking, floating and relaxing but all exuding love.

"You see, Mary-Anne," the black-faced cuckoo-shrike said, "here is every person you have helped in one way or another. From family members to ex-lovers to work colleagues to strangers on the street you have given directions or money.

"Every person you have shown love to indirectly or directly is in this room. All the people you have positively influenced in your life have benefited in one way or another.

"For some, it may have been a simple drink to quench their

thirst; for others, it might have been money to pay the rent; and for some, it may have been helpful advice that changed their heart and mind to focus on positive energy, not negative energy.

"You have touched many people in this life so far, Mary-Anne, and have had a great influence."

Mary-Anne couldn't stop smiling and just wanted to hug and be hugged.

But the black-faced cuckoo-shrike wasn't finished yet.

"This, however, is the past, Mary-Anne," it said with a serious voice. "All this love you have given is only the tip of the iceberg to prepare you for the next stage of your life.

"The role you are to play in life is far greater than the one you have played so far. All the mistakes and lessons you have learned in your past you need to take heed of and store in your memory.

"You are now free to move forward. Your responsibilities are there for you now to shed in your current life. You need to extricate yourself from your current life and free your mind, body and soul for what is about to transpire.

"Your inner energy will start to glow, and soon, a new lease of life will come upon you, but this can happen only if you let go of the past. Each day that you resist letting go means a day further away from your enlightenment. It is up to you how fast and how slow you move from here, but you know your life is out of balance.

"But be warned: you won't be happy while you are a slave to modern riches, as they destroy your soul. Once you have found peace within, your talents will be recognised, the greater the love you will give and receive, and the more fulfilled in your life you will be."

Upon hearing the last sentence, she looked around to see the beach in the distance and the oak tree nearby.

Mary-Anne found herself staring straight at the oak tree. She walked straight up to it, gave it a kiss and hugged the tree for what seemed an eternity. This wasn't a hug of sorrow and self-pity like yesterday's but a hug of love.

Day 6: Friday
(New love)

Before she had gone to bed the night before, Mary-Anne had decided to turn her alarm off. She wanted to sleep naturally.

She fell asleep easily and woke mid-morning.

Mary-Anne had never felt so peaceful and so rested. It was as if she had spent the night in heaven. She had dreamed vividly and peacefully. Not a bone or muscle in her body ached. She looked outside, and on the last day of spring, the sun was shining with a gentle breeze blowing. It looked like a beautiful day.

Mary-Anne turned her phone on, not to answer any work calls, emails or texts but to call one person – her new love. She had been thinking of him all week but had not contacted him.

She rang her new love, and he answered the phone immediately. Within a minute, they were laughing and five minutes later, they had arranged to meet in one hour. She decided that was enough of her phone today. She wouldn't go into work. She wouldn't respond to any work messages, and she wouldn't think about it for the rest of the day.

She showered at leisure and then, for the first time all week, ate breakfast sitting out at the back of her sister's house by the pool, watching as the wind rustled the leaves in the trees.

She felt serene.

Mary-Anne headed to meet her new love, and they spent a wonderful day together talking, laughing, eating, hugging and making love. They fell asleep late in the afternoon in the park, but when Mary-Anne awoke, her new love was nowhere to be seen.

She looked around and started to search for him, when she suddenly saw a grey butcherbird land on a bench in front of her.

It was a distinctive bird with a black crown and face, a grey back and a thin white collar. The wings were grey with large areas of white all over its body.

All of a sudden, the bird started to sing – and, boy, could it sing – and for the first time all week, the bird was not alone. The male and female were together, and they were singing in harmony and in full voice.

Mary-Anne suddenly couldn't stop singing herself. She was laughing, singing, whistling and dancing. She felt crazy. She felt free. She felt in love. She felt it was, at last, how it should be.

The grey butcherbirds sang in harmony, with the male starting the whistling and the female joining in. It was as if Mary-Anne knew every theme and felt as though she was walking on clouds.

And then, in a flash, they flew off into the sky. Mary-Anne looked down and saw the beach in front of her eyes.

But instead of scurrying along to see the boy, she stood still and felt the cool breeze upon her face. She picked up a handful of sand and let it fall between her fingers and then squished it between her toes.

She stripped naked and dived into the ocean, swimming out to sea and then catching a wave back in. She enjoyed it so much, she did it again and again, all the time laughing merrily along, singing, humming and whistling.

Eventually, Mary-Anne caught a wave right into the shore and stood naked in the sun, drying off. She felt reborn. She couldn't remember being more contented.

Once dry, she dressed herself and started walking down the beach, looking for the boy. He seemed to be farther away today, as she still couldn't see him. But she wasn't worried, as she knew he would come into sight soon enough. She would enjoy the sun, the sea and the breeze until that moment arrived, all the while singing out loud.

Soon enough, the boy came into sight. The blue-eyed, blond, scruffy-haired boy wearing the white shorts and yellow T-shirt was standing back from his sandcastle. He was looking very serious.

"What's wrong?" Mary-Anne asked.

"Nothing," said the boy. "Sometimes you just need to stand back from something you are close to in order to really appreciate what you have."

"Very profound," Mary-Anne replied. "You have wisdom beyond your years."

The boy didn't respond but went back to attending to his sandcastle.

"You will see my latest room is at the top of the castle," the boy said matter-of-factly. "It is possible to see from every angle. There is nothing blocking its view of the air, the sea and the land. It is the best room in the castle. Everyone wants to be in this room."

The castle was so tall now that Mary-Anne hardly had to bend down.

She looked in the biggest and highest room of the castle and immediately saw her new love. She saw them dancing together, laughing, talking day and night, cuddling each other, eating together, and sharing many wonderful moments. She saw her inner soul light up, and her heart beat faster.

"You have finally met your match," the two grey butcherbirds said. "Your new love has the ability to set you free from your past. He can help heal your wounds and help you discover what truly makes you happy. He is here to take you to the next phase of your life, and he will continue that journey with you."

Mary-Anne nodded, as if she already knew that but for some reason had been fighting it.

"So why, then, do you challenge what the universe has given you?" the two grey butcherbirds said in unison. "When you feel sad, doesn't he make you feel happy? When you feel like crying, doesn't he make you laugh? When you feel tired, doesn't he make you want to stay awake? When you feel listless, doesn't he make you want to break out in song?

"How can you question the love you feel for someone and the love someone gives to you, when every time you have a negative emotion about to override your mind and body, that person counteracts it with a positive emotion?

"Sure, he is not perfect, and there is no perfect compatibility in the human universe, but he is as compatible a person as you will meet in this life, and that is not to say you may have met before in another time and place."

Mary-Anne knew this to be true. All year she had questioned why someone with so much energy would appear in her life when she just wanted to spend her time in despair. She wanted to weep, sleep, feel sorry for herself and retreat from the world. Yet she was drawn to this enigmatic person and felt a natural connection to him.

"Unfortunately in today's world, we are all so sceptical of why something positive is happening to us," the two butcherbirds said together. "We feel as though we don't deserve, or we aren't worthy, when in fact each of us deserves goodness and love in our life.

"We also tend to believe that no one can love us for our faults and insecurities, but the fact is, if we were perfect, we would be harder to love.

"Love comes in all shapes and sizes and at various times of our life. One should not discount it, no matter what mood we are in or what we think we should experience.

"The universe has given you love this year, but you question its motives. Do you think you know more than the universe?"

At this point, Mary-Anne looked sheepish.

"Embrace this new love and let him help guide you to find true enlightenment. You have spent enough years in the dark. Aren't you happy that someone finally turned the light on?"

And in an instant, the two grey butcherbirds were gone.

Mary-Anne found herself lying under the oak tree. The roots had formed a comfortable base for her to sleep on, with a nice groove in the stump to rest her head on. The leaves had fallen together and were spread like a blanket. The oak tree extended its branches to shade her from the sun, and the sea breeze was so light as if not to disturb her but to give her comfort that life all around her was continuing.

Day 7: Saturday
(The present)

Mary-Anne awoke on the Saturday, and it was the first day of summer. All week, the weather had been blissful, with sunny days and light winds. Today looked like no exception.

Mary-Anne again woke naturally with no buzzing and loud alarm to disturb her soul. Technology is killing our senses, she thought. But today, she didn't wake in her sister's house but in her lover's bed. It was a funny bed, a bit like his personality, a mix of the old century and the new. A complex man, she thought, but no more complex than she.

Mary-Anne decided to go for a walk while he slept and knew that a bakery was nearby. She was whistling along when she saw a new holland honeyeater feeding on the nectar of a blossoming tree. It was happily eating when it saw Mary-Anne approaching.

The new holland honeyeater swallowed the nectar and the insect in his mouth and nodded for Mary-Anne to follow. She smiled and, for some reason, felt like skipping. She skipped and laughed while watching the new holland honeyeater dipping out of the sky into trees and eating insects as they fell.

It was an attractive bird that was predominantly black and white with a large yellow wing patch and yellow sides on the tail. Soon, like the rainbow lorikeet, the noisy miner, the yellow robin, the satin bowerbird, the black-faced cuckoo shrike and the grey butcherbirds, it disappeared into the sky, on to its next journey.

Mary-Anne was once again at the beach. This time, she decided to take a nap on the sand. She felt calm and wanted to enjoy the sunshine. Just as she lay down, the sun went behind the clouds and the wind eased.

She awoke some time later, and was surprised to find the blue-eyed blond boy standing over her.

"Come on," he said excitedly. "I've finished. I have been waiting for you all day."

The boy held out his hand and grabbed Mary-Anne's, and then they started running down the beach. She was surprised that the boy in the white shorts and yellow T-shirt was so strong and quick.

Before she knew it, they were at the castle, and it was an impressive sight. The castle had seven storeys, with each storey dedicated to one room. But the storeys did not sit on top of each other; they expanded and entwined in a maze with a surrounding wall all around and vantage points at each corner.

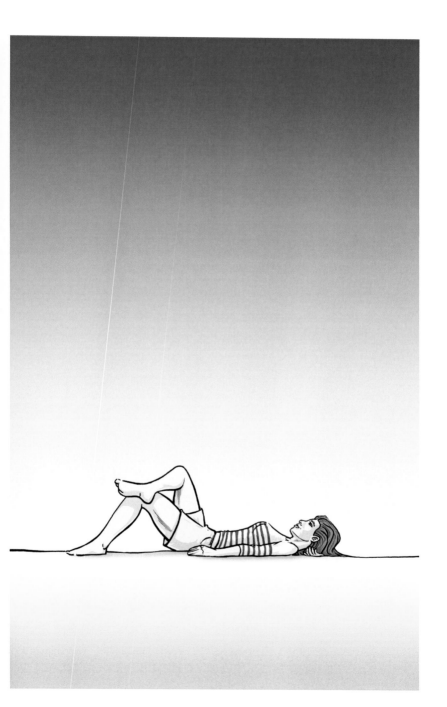

The water from the ocean flowed into the perimeter, creating a place for people to bathe, and a filter had been set up to extract the salt to provide drinking water.

There were windmills built to generate power and clear walking areas for everyone to get to anywhere at any given time. In some ways, it was a labyrinth; in other ways, not.

It was aesthetically pleasing, to say the least, and the design was as creative as that of any sandcastle built.

Mary-Anne had no doubt that there were secret tunnels running throughout and maybe even a passage out of the castle leading up to the oak tree. If her imagination were running wild, what would be going on in the mind of a little boy?

She looked across and saw he was very content with his work. His arms were folded across his yellow T-shirt and his white shorts were covered in sand.

"The last room is the most interesting," the boy said. "I am sure you will find many things there to make you ponder."

The boy looked at Mary-Anne, and she looked back. She had a feeling that she wouldn't see the boy again, so before she looked into the window of the seventh room, she walked across and hugged him. Slowly, but surely, the boy accepted the hug and eventually unfolded his arms and hugged Mary-Anne back.

"May I ask you one question?" Mary-Anne asked, standing back from the boy.

The boy didn't move. "Who are you?"

The boy simply smiled, and for the first time all week, Mary-Anne saw the boy leave.

She then gently gazed into the window of the finest and most extravagant room sitting on top of the castle and saw her life flash before her eyes. All significant moments appeared and disappeared, and people who had impacted her came and went too.

There were different houses, places, countries, cars, jobs and everything that Mary-Anne had deemed important in her life.

But after they had all come and gone, she was faced with a big question mark.

It was at this moment that the new holland honeyeater flew inside the room and perched on top of the question mark.

"The day has come for you to make up your mind," the honeyeater said. "Today and in the past six days, you have seen all your life come before you. Some painful times, some happy, some sad, some glad. Everything of significance has been presented to remind you of who you have been, but more importantly, who you are.

"But today is the day you get to make a choice about

what you want to do with your life. You have reached the crossroads. You can continue to be caught up in the world that makes you fundamentally unhappy with all its greed, neediness, demands and shallowness, or you can simply start your life again by exiting from your past and moving forward.

"Human beings who are caught up in living today and regretting yesterday never see beyond tomorrow. They don't seek spiritual enlightenment or happiness because they are consumed with what is important now to them, not to anyone else."

Mary-Anne was very pensive.

"Half of your life has gone, and it has been a great learning experience," the new holland honeyeater said. "You are a wonderful, beautiful human being with so much to give, but you misplace your energy. It is caught up in a greedy world where people lose sight of the goodness of others and the simple things that make them happy. You are above that.

"Human beings are meant to be at peace with one another and embrace the natural beauty of nature all around. We are not meant to spend our life accumulating assets, fighting, destroying our natural land, ignoring our neighbour, and coveting materialistic gifts that benefit no one but ourselves.

"You can help change the destruction in the world by showing the way with your natural touch and light, encouraging all around you to see the goodness in others.

"Your natural light has been diminished, but you have been given the opportunity this year to see a slight glimpse of how different your future could be.

"You have new love in your life and the freedom to achieve any task that you want. It is only your belief in an old and decaying society that is holding you back. You can start again and use your light and healing powers to help others. No one is fully healed, but by showering light, kindness and help upon others, our soul transforms, and we become someone we should be and can be.

"You have light, love and hope in your heart and mind. Use that power to spread the word that when one person wants to positively influence the world, others will follow."

And with those final words, the new holland honeyeater flew off into the clouds.

Mary-Anne walked over to the oak tree for one last time. She walked all around the tree and then climbed its branches. Each branch took her higher, and upon each branch, she looked both down and around at the earth.

She eventually climbed high among the branches where all of the eight birds were sitting together – the rainbow lorikeet, the noisy miner, the yellow robin, the satin bowerbird, the black-faced cuckoo-shrike, the two grey butcherbirds and the new holland honeyeater – all singing along merrily.

They barely noticed Mary-Anne, for she was one of them now. She started to hum along with the birds, as if it was where she always belonged – on top of the tree – at one with nature, feeling the wind, embracing the sun, and watching the sea from an entirely different angle.

Day 8: Sunday
(The future)

For the third day in a row, Mary-Anne woke naturally, and for the first time in her adult working life, she decided that she wasn't going to turn on her phone. She waited for her lover to wake up, and they made the most intense, passionate love of their lives.

Afterwards, when he napped, she looked at him, up and down. Yes, he had faults, and, yes, he wasn't perfect, but he was perfect for her, and she was perfect for him. Together, they would work as a team and build a way forward.

For twelve months she had resisted her love for him and refused to let herself fall in love, convincing herself that it couldn't happen to her and that she wasn't worthy. She had multiplied his weaknesses so as to discount his strengths and preyed upon every slip of the tongue and hurtful gesture that he made.

But she had been hopelessly drawn to him from the beginning, unable to prise herself away even through the difficult times. He was the first person she called when sick, scared, happy or unprepared. They had a connection from the outset, unlike any other she had experienced.

She had fought his love but now no longer felt that way. She was prepared to give in and let this man, her closest companion in her life, be with her in mind, body and spirit.

As her partner was sleeping, Mary-Anne decided to go for a walk. She wanted a coffee. Old habits die hard, she thought.

As she walked, she started to wonder if a new bird would appear today. She walked farther and farther, thinking that she must see a bird, but none appeared. After all, we all want guidance in our lives, and Mary-Anne was no different.

She wanted comfort; she wanted the beach and the little boy building his sandcastle.

Soon, Mary-Anne started to run. She didn't know where she was running to, but somehow, she hoped that a bird would appear and give her guidance.

Yet there were no birds today of any description and no secret beach to be found.

Mary-Anne started to panic and cry.

She needed more guidance. What would happen to her if things didn't work out? What would she do if she quit her job and sold her assets? Who would help her in times of need?

All these negative thoughts ran through her head, as they do in most humans when confronted with change.

Mary-Anne stopped, stood still and caught her breath. She breathed slowly and deliberately. She realised that she had been taught many lessons in the past seven days and had been given spiritual guidance for her life to move forward in many different ways.

She had been blessed by the universe but once again was questioning its judgement. She felt guilty. She looked up to heaven and thanked God for the gifts of the past week.

She started to walk back home with her head down and feeling sorry for herself, but with each step, her head slowly rose, and soon she was appreciating the second day of summer and all the joy that summer brings.

Her frown turned into a smile. She started to sing and laugh out loud in the street, addressing each stranger on the way with a genuine greeting. She noticed that with each "hello" or "good morning", each person's demeanour changed, and they were all smiling upon encountering her.

She felt secure as she returned to her boyfriend's house and looked forward to seeing him. She called out his name, but there was no answer, and soon she saw a note on the kitchen table saying that he had gone for a run.

How ironic, she thought.

Mary-Anne took a bath, put on her dressing gown and started to make lunch. As the food was cooking, she put on some music and started to look through the bookshelves.

She had never really paid much attention to what kind of books her boyfriend read and was fascinated to see what eclectic taste he had. There were both fiction and non-fiction, novels, books on history, autobiographies, university texts, sports and language books.

He had three full bookcases spanning two rooms. As she reached the bottom of the third bookcase, she found a photo album. This should be interesting, she thought, as I don't know a lot of his past.

She retreated back to the sofa and placed the photo album next to her. She poured a glass of wine and turned to pick up the photo album, noticing she had opened it from the back.

It wasn't her intention to start from the back of the photo album, but she thought, Well, this is where the book opened, so I shall start from here.

She looked at pictures of him out with friends, on holiday overseas, with ex-girlfriends (she lingered a bit too long on these), of family, of weddings, of his university days and his school years.

Mary-Anne thought he had changed over the years, but there was something familiar about his face.

As she turned to the very first page of his photo album, she dropped the glass of red wine onto the carpet of the loungeroom floor.

There she saw a picture of a blue-eyed, blond boy, wearing a yellow T-shirt and white shorts, standing on a beach next to a magnificent sandcastle.

If Love, then What?

By Louis White

Chapter One

In all his excitement, Joshua had forgotten one important fact. Was Mrs Macquarie's Chair an actual chair in the Royal Botanic Gardens or was it simply a generic meeting place?

Despite being born in Sydney, Joshua had never been there, which was partly the reason for doing so today, because he wanted it to be special.

In his excitement of arranging to meet up, he had forgotten to look up exactly where Mrs Macquarie's Chair was.

He checked his phone but there was no signal. Bloody telecommunications providers were still useless as ever even though it was 2022. He walked upstairs to the top of the ferry and pointed his phone to the highest point of the sky, but there was still no signal.

"Why don't you just enjoy the scenery around you?" a younger, know-it-all passenger quipped.

Joshua looked him up and down—too much product in his hair, ridiculous man bag, trousers too short, unoriginal sleeve tattoo, necklace, designer shirt matching his boat shoes, coupled with leaning across two seats as if he was cool—tosser.

"If I wanted your opinion, I would have asked for it," Joshua stated, walking towards the tosser before holding his gaze and staring him down.

The tosser retreated into his shell and looked away. Joshua walked downstairs to the back of the ferry. He checked the time on his phone.

"Fuck!" He unintentionally said it out loud. He was running late thanks to that one moronic car driver travelling fifteen kilometres under the speed limit and virtually stopping at every green light. Why did people do that? Slow down when they saw a green light? It always baffled him.

This caused him to miss the earlier ferry.

There was no signal on his phone, so he couldn't even make contact.

Waiting patiently wasn't one of Joshua's strong points. His mind was always ahead of his speech. Often in his head, he had already finished a sentence and was starting the next one before he had completed the last three or four words of the first sentence.

People often stared at him with some confusion when they first heard him speak because he spoke too fast, and he found himself slowing down for a sentence or two to let them catch up before he reverted to normal. He couldn't help who he was, nor did he wish to, or believe he could, change.

He didn't care whether people fully understood him or not. Sooner or later, he would be speaking to someone else, so it didn't really matter. In his profession, you were meeting new people all the time, and they were only as useful as the information they provided.

He had plenty of friends who knew and understood him. That was enough.

In what seemed an eternity, but in reality was only five minutes, the ferry docked at Circular Quay. Joshua manoeuvred his way to the front of the queue before walking in haste towards the Opera House.

Even though it was only 25 degrees, Joshua could feel the sweat beginning to build. That was the Sydney humidity. It was there all year round. Great, what an impression he would make.

There was no way of avoiding the sun, and on days like this, he wished his head had a natural affinity with hats. For some reason, they were like distant cousins, more comfortable apart.

He stopped briefly on the steps of the Opera House when he felt his phone buzzing.

The text read: "Running late, be there very soon. Can't wait. XX"

Normally, that would send Joshua into a frenzy, as he hated people texting five minutes before they were supposed to be somewhere stating that they were running late. In his mind, you obviously knew you were going to be late more than five minutes before you sent the text.

But today was different. Today was special. God, he hoped it was.

One problem still remained. Where the hell was Mrs Macquarie's Chair? He looked it up on his phone, but that presented another problem. Despite seeing an image of the chair, Joshua had no sense of direction. His sense of geography was so bad, he could seriously get lost on a football field.

He consulted the map near the entrance of the Royal Botanic Gardens, but that didn't help either. Why didn't he just drive? Hindsight was always a blessing in disguise. Joshua was now confronted with another of his pet hates— talking to the general public.

"Excuse me. Do you know exactly where Mrs Macquarie's Chair is?" he politely asked a young couple.

They pulled out a map and in their strong German accents replied, "It is in the Domain near the Royal Botanic Gardens."

"What? The Domain? That's ages away. Fuck me."

"Yes. According to this guide, it will take you twenty minutes to walk there."

"Danke," Joshua replied and walked off before stopping ten seconds later.

Joshua was frazzled. His head was spinning. He was hot and annoyed at himself. He was already ten minutes late, and sweat was dripping down the side of his face. Awesome. All he needed to do now was to bump into a tourist eating an ice cream to stain his shirt to complete the dishevelment.

He saw the silly little train that was taking people on tours of the Royal Botanic Gardens, and he thought he would jump on—the Choo Choo Express—but before he parted with his ten dollars, he had one question to ask the overweight and disinterested employee sitting behind a cheap table staring at her phone as if it provided oxygen.

Joshua waited impatiently for her to look up but soon realised that was never going to happen.

"Excuse me. Does this train go to Mrs Macquarie's Chair?"

"No," came the abrupt reply.

Not once did her eyes leave her phone.

Joshua started walking. He looked at his phone and decided not to communicate. He would try to cut the time down from twenty minutes to fifteen without sweating too much.

Was that possible?

He wasn't sure, but nevertheless, he would try.

Luckily, a slight breeze had picked up and the cloud cover had started to increase. If his Year 9 geography class lesson served him well, they were stratocumulus clouds, and no rain was in sight.

For reasons unknown to Joshua, he always remembered the lessons on cloud formations and cloud types, even though they had taken place more than three decades ago.

Maybe it was because the teacher, Mr Jansen, in his strong Dutch accent, went to such great pains to draw the different types of clouds on the board and pass around pictures, or maybe it was because it was the only aspect of geography that Joshua found interesting.

For some reason, maps bored him and looked like hard work. Despite having extensively travelled around the world in his adult life, Joshua still had no interest in looking at maps at any time or in trying to read them.

Trying to understand latitude and longitude was the equivalent of learning a new language.

Joshua looked at the curve in the path and realised that in a straight line he could make the destination in half the time, but that wasn't possible because he couldn't walk on water.

Where was that speedboat when you needed it?

He looked around at the children playing in the gardens and families carrying their picnic baskets. Yes, he had picked the right location for this date, if that was what it was. Joshua didn't really know.

As Joshua neared his destination, he received another text. "I'm here. Where are you? Can't wait much longer. I am dying with excitement. XXXX."

Joshua suddenly became aware of what he was wearing. Am I underdressed?

He was wearing a brand-new blue-and-white short-sleeve collared shirt he had just purchased from Reiss Menswear, khaki shorts from Industrie, and some marine-blue casual shoes from Allbirds. He was even wearing brand-new black Armani boxers.

Every single item of this clothing had been purchased the day before. Well, besides his Persol sunglasses, which he had purchased in Italy and which, although slightly bent, felt perfect on his face.

He could feel his heart beating faster. Was this a mistake? What did he really expect was going to happen today? That he would fall in love and start his life again?

Joshua reached another curve and walked up the stairs. He looked at the photo on the website to confirm he was at the right destination.

"Excuse me. Do you know exactly where Mrs Macquarie's Chair is?"

A youngish couple looked at each other.

"I think here somewhere," the cute Spanish girl said. Was this international tourist day?

He looked down at the rocks and watched a professional photographer shooting with a long lens towards the Opera House.

Joshua looked up and saw a traditional bench. That can't be it, he thought. Mrs Macquarie's Chair looks as if it's carved from sandstone.

Joshua was unsure of whether to walk around the bend or walk slightly up the hill. Despite being a very decisive person in his everyday life who relished the opportunity to make big decisions, he found situations like this confusing and irritating.

He just wanted the answer now!

"Excuse me. Do you know exactly where Mrs Macquarie's Chair is?"

The jogger took off her headphones. "Sorry. Can you repeat the question?" she said, jogging on the spot as if it made a difference.

"Do you know exactly where Mrs Macquarie's Chair is?" Joshua had to refrain from saying it sarcastically.

"Just keep walking. You can't miss it."

"Okay, thanks."

Joshua took a deep breath. He needed to calm down. He was standing in the shade of the trees, and the breeze felt divine.

He slowed his walk as he felt his body starting to shake.

He couldn't believe how nervous he was. He was starting to have doubts.

Then, just as he was having second, and third, and fourth doubtful thoughts and contemplated turning back, he looked up and caught a glimpse of the love of his life.

The smile on his face had never been broader.

Chapter Two

Jasmine looked in the mirror one last time—for the hundredth time. She was convinced that she didn't look pretty at all. How could she? After all she had been through…

She no longer had the wrinkle-free face or the body she used to possess when she was a triathlete, though she could still swim a kilometre in good time or run ten kilometres in relative comfort, which was encouraging, given those chances were rare in her current circumstances. For the last three months, she had been training hard—but not for a triathlon—to look good today.

But, still, knowing she could do it was comfort enough. Well, it had to be; otherwise, life became too depressing. That escape, that time alone, competing against no one but herself, was the one aspect of her life that she clung onto and made her feel as though she still had control.

If she lost that, then getting up in the morning would become almost impossible. 'Keep something for yourself' was what her mother had always said. Always remember to keep something for yourself that will allow you to feel as though your sense of self-worth and belonging to yourself remained intact.

Exercise was her outlet as her career was so encompassing. She had worked in the healthcare business all her life.

Executive sales was demanding but extremely financially rewarding, especially when it came to selling pharmaceutical goods. That was a licence to print money. Still, it wasn't exactly saving lives and left Jasmine feeling a little bit hollow at times. At some stage, she would re-evaluate her career. But not right now.

She could do it. She had to keep telling herself to push on through despite everything else confronting her.

Jasmine looked down at her Cartier watch.

"Fuck!" How long had she been daydreaming? Now, she was really going to be late. She had better text. Luckily, she was staying in the city, so it wasn't far to go.

Make-up, hair, nails all done. Legs, top lip and vagina waxed. Underarms shaved and good to go.

She laid out her Victoria's Secret underwear on the bed. She hadn't worn sexy underwear for as long as she could remember, but who knew what might happen today?

As she slowly first put on her thong and then her bra, the feel of it was surreal, and she was glad she had been to the gym almost every day for the past three months in preparation for this catch-up. Or was it a date?

The thong and bra set felt amazingly comfortable, and her D-cup breasts still had some life in them. Her bum didn't look too bad either, and those thousands of squats and lunges had put her legs in great shape. They were toned with some definition. Just the right balance.

God, she was excited. Finally, getting to meet. Finally!

She'd thought this day would never happen. Jasmine was staring at herself in her full-length mirror, turning side on and then trying to swivel her head to look at her bum and legs. This way and then that.

God, she was so horny, but that would have to wait. She looked down at her watch.

"Fuck me!"

She quickly put on her Dolce & Gabbana floral dress, grabbed her Gucci handbag, eased into Versace heels and exited her room for the lift. She was just about to leave when she remembered her Prada sunglasses were still in the bathroom.

Waiting impatiently, she smiled at the elderly couple looking her up and down on the seventh floor, to which the woman commented, "Going on a date at this time of the day? That sounds exciting!"

Jasmine said, "Something like that."

"Oh, that's an interesting accent. Where are you from?"

The lift door opened, and they were confronted by a horde of children. Jasmine decided to wait but waved to the elderly couple as they entered.

"Enjoy your day," she said politely and found herself waving inexplicably like the Queen of England. Jasmine giggled at herself.

Suddenly, there was a ping, and the corresponding lift arrived. Luckily, this was empty.

The lift descended quickly, and Jasmine once again looked at herself up and down in the lift mirror.

Was she vain or just nervous? Probably both, but who cared?

The lift opened, and she walked straight past reception into a waiting cab.

"Mrs Macquarie's Chair please."

The taxi driver didn't move his head from staring at his phone. "You know you can walk there."

"I know, but I would prefer if you drove me there."

The taxi driver grumbled to himself, threw his phone onto the passenger seat and then took off abruptly. And the taxi industry wondered why people preferred Uber.

Jasmine checked her phone, and there had been no reply.

What did that mean? Was she going to be stood up? Surely not. Not after all this time, but maybe that could happen.

Maybe it didn't matter to him. Would he really do that? Stand her up? Was all this ridiculous? Had she put way too much thought into today?

She opened up her handbag and pulled out her compact and looked at herself once again.

She could feel a drop of sweat running down her back into her thong. Surprisingly, she didn't mind. She loved sweaty pulsating sex. It was another form of exercise but far more enjoyable.

Sex. Oh my God, it had been so long. She craved it. She could feel it swirl within her. She just had to control herself, but if she didn't get fucked soon, she would go crazy.

She began thinking about who she would like to have sex with right then.

It was hard not to touch herself, but she had to resist. She was in a taxi, for God's sake.

The taxi stopped. "We're here."

"Where exactly is Mrs Macquarie's Chair?"

"Just over there." The taxi driver pointed with his thick fingers. "You can't miss it."

Jasmine gave the taxi driver twenty dollars. "Keep the change."

He grunted again. Never once did he turn around to look at her. That was his loss, as he realised when he picked up his phone from the passenger seat and looked up to see this stunning buxom brunette walking past his front passenger door and on to her rendezvous.

"I can't believe I didn't talk to her!" the taxi driver shouted out loud, beeping his horn in frustration. Soon, the cars behind were doing the same, as he was holding up traffic, but he sat motionless, reflecting upon his stupidity.

"Fuck off," he screamed, turning his head and driving off quicker than he needed to.

Jasmine started walking slowly to Mrs Macquarie's Chair. There was no one there, which was surprising.

Was he going to turn up? She was suddenly full of doubts. She sent another text.

Was that over the top? She didn't think so.

She waited nervously.

Walkers, joggers and various interested parties were coming and going in all directions.

Everyone seemed happy. Blue sky seemed to have that effect.

How lovely was Sydney? How lucky people were to live here.

Jasmine could get used to it. She certainly didn't see much blue sky where she was from.

The setting couldn't have been any prettier. Was today going to be perfect?

Her heart was pounding a million beats a minute. She looked to her right and then to her left.

Which direction?

Calm down, she thought.

Then suddenly, she saw a figure approaching.

She knew that walk, that smile, that face, that body. God, he looked better now than when they last met—

almost twenty years ago.

Her heart just wanted to burst with love, lust, pride and exhilaration all at once.

She ran as quickly as her heels would let her.

White Tiger

MEDIA
PRODUCTIONS

LOUIS WHITE
Director

**White Tiger
Media Productions Pty Ltd**
Level 57, MLC Centre
19-29 Martin Place
Sydney, NSW 2000

p: +61 2 9238 2085
e: louis.white@whitetigermedia.com.au
w: www.whitetigermedia.com.au

**Children's books published
by White Tiger Media**

Blue Skies for Lily
Lily and the Butterfly
A Christmas Story
Lily and the Dragon
Lily and the Ant

**Adult books published
by White Tiger Media**

Sandcastles
One Season
If love, then what?

To order a copy of *If Love, then What?*
by Louis White
please email
info@whitetigermedia.com.au